This igloo book belongs to:

....

igloobooks

Published in 2018
by Igloo Books Ltd
Cottage Farm
Sywell
NN6 0BJ
www.igloobooks.com

STA002 0418
2 4 6 8 10 9 7 5 3
ISBN 978-1-78440-421-5

Illustrated by Kathryn Durst
Written by Charlie Griffin

Designed by Matthew Ellero
Edited by Jenny Cox

Printed and manufactured in China

the Boy who Said NO!

igloobooks

When Max was a baby,
he was all
SWEETNESS
and LIGHT.

His mum and dad adored him and
they cuddled him tight.

Then Max grew **bigger** and things began to change.

Mum and Dad noticed
something quite strange.

When it happened, Mum and Dad didn't quite know.
It was just that one day, Max began to say...

Before long, it was the only word Max had to say.
He said it more than a hundred times a day.

If Mum said,
"Come on, Max.
Get up, let's go."

Max clung to Teddy
and just said...

Max refused to get out of bed.

NO!

... he cried.

"I'm staying **here** instead."

It was...

NO!

... to T-shirts.

NO!

... to shoes.

It was...

NO!

... to everything
Mum would choose.

At mealtimes, Max was always in a bad mood.

NO!

... he said.

"I don't like **any** of that food!"

When he really should have been in bed,
Max refused and shook his head.

"Relax, Max," said Mum. "Go with the flow."
Max stamped his feet and **shouted**...

The next day, Mum didn't wake Max.
She woke up Teddy instead.

"Let's get you dressed, Teddy.
I've got a surprise," **she said.**

"If only Max could get dressed, too, he would come along with you."

Max didn't want to be left behind.
He quickly got dressed and he didn't mind.

At breakfast, Mum pretended Teddy had eaten all his up.
"So have I!" said Max, finishing the milk from his cup.

"It's time for the surprise," said Mum.
"Well done, Teddy."

"I want the surprise, too!"
cried Max. "I'm all ready."

"What is it?" asked Max, as they got in the car.

"Will it take long?"

"Is it very far?"

It seemed like ages, until Dad stopped somewhere...

... right outside the
mega funfair!

Welcome!

Mum put Teddy by Max's side.
She asked if Max would like to go on a ride.

Max's reply wasn't hard to guess.
Suddenly, he became the boy who said...